This book is presented to families
participating in SAFEchild's PLUS Program
by
Mr. Andy Smith

in memory of his father,
the author,
Mr. Wayne Smith

2005

THE FOUR BEARS

Story by Wayne Smith ❧ Illustrations by Irene Salokin

LONGSTREET PRESS, INC.
Atlanta, Georgia

Published by Longstreet Press, Inc.
A subsidiary of Cox Newspapers,
A subsidiary of Cox Enterprises, Inc.
2140 Newmarket Parkway
Suite 118
Marietta, GA 30067

Printed in the United States of America
1st printing, 1995

Library of Congress Catalog Card Number: 95-77259
ISBN 1-56352-237-3

Jacket and book design by Jill Dible
Electronic film prep and separations by Advertising Technologies, Inc., Atlanta, GA

This book is dedicated to the world's most patient and forgiving woman, my wife Carolyn, and to our two grandchildren, James and Jessica.

THE FOUR BEARS

Not so long ago, in a log cabin in the middle of a thick forest, there lived a bear family. Their forest stood in a faraway land that lay over the ocean and was called Siberia.

Boris the Bear was the head of the bear family. He was a loving husband to his wife, Olga, and a caring father to their two bear cubs. The cubs were Tanya, who was thirteen years old, and her younger brother, Ivan, a five-year-old who was fond of mischief.

The trees around the bears' home were high and mighty. As you looked around, you saw nothing but trees. But among the trees, the forest was full of animals and birds. They were the bears' friends.

Very early one morning, Tanya and Ivan awoke and saw a small bird in the fir tree outside their window. They watched him hop from one branch to another.

"Good morning, Mr. Bird," said Ivan. The bird looked down at the two bears and cocked its head. Ivan and Tanya were happy they could speak the language of the birds. They also could speak Russian, the language of Siberia. In fact, they could speak every language under the sun. Ivan and Tanya and Boris and Olga were magic bears.

Later that morning, Olga, the Bear Mother, asked her two cubs if they would like to go to Silver Lake, beyond the White Mountains, to gather raspberries. "Look," she said, "it's such a wonderful morning, and the sun is bright and lovely. I'm sure there will be plenty of your favorite raspberries to pick. What do you think, Tanya and Ivan? Shall we go?"

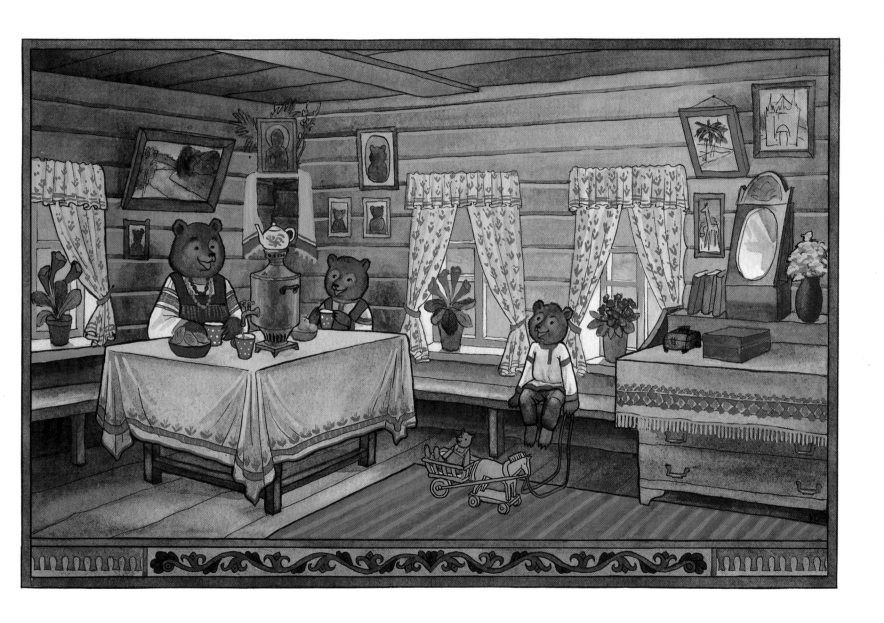

Of course they wanted to go! But, could Father go along with them?

"Will you go with us, Daddy?" Tanya and Ivan asked eagerly.

"No," said Boris. "I'd like to join you, but I can't. I have some work to do today, and it's very important."

"What kind of work is it?" asked little Ivan, who was always asking questions.

"Some of us forest bears promised Peter, the new Forest Ranger, that we would help him clear away some fallen trees. Many trees fell during last week's storm," Boris explained.

Ivan remembered how much fun he had tromping through the forest and picking raspberries with his father.

"Can't you tell the Forest Ranger you are busy and come along with us, instead?" Ivan suggested.

"Busy, you say?" Boris grunted in reply. "Do you want me to break my word? Don't you know that a promise, once made, should be kept?" Of course Ivan knew that . . . but he so badly wanted his father to go with them.

"I will make a different promise to you, one that I will also keep," said Boris as he picked Ivan up and set him on his knee. "Before the end of the summer, I will go with you to pick raspberries." Then Ivan was happy, because he knew he would go with his father another day.

So Boris kissed the others good-bye and left for work while the two bear cubs and their mother set off for Silver Lake. Olga and Tanya walked slowly and talked together, but Ivan skipped ahead. He could hardly wait to taste the bright red raspberries!

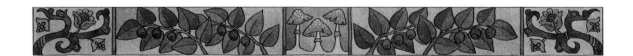

It was a long walk to Silver Lake, but when they got there, oh, how beautiful everything was! They sat for a moment and gazed at Silver Lake and the White Mountains beyond.

Raspberry picking was not all fun. By the time their wicker baskets were full, Olga and Tanya were tired. Meanwhile, Ivan was so curious to explore the forest that he wasn't watching where he was going. He tripped over a clump of grass, and his berries spilled from his basket!

The evening sun was going down, and Olga decided it was time to go home. She took Ivan's basket along with her own, and off the bears went down the path that snaked through the woods. Little did Olga and Tanya realize that Ivan, who brought up the rear, was lagging much too far behind. The little bear cub still wanted to explore. He couldn't resist leaving the path every now and then to play with the brown cones scattered on the ground. Sometimes he wandered among the fir trees. Now and again, he pretended to be talking with a friend.

By the time Olga and Tanya looked around, the bear cub was nowhere in sight. Poor Ivan had stumbled into a deep hole and could not get out.

His mother and his sister did not hear Ivan's desperate cries for help. They were too far away.

"Mama! Tanya!" he called. But he heard only the echo of his own voice in the deep forest.

Peter the Forest Ranger had finished working with the forest bears and was on his way home when he heard Ivan's cries. In one minute Peter reached the hole and saw the trapped bear cub. He thrust his long arm down and helped little Ivan climb out. Ivan had never been happier to see anyone. He noticed that Peter was as happy as he was. Helping someone made Peter feel needed.

No sooner had Peter dusted Ivan's fur coat and stroked his head than Boris appeared on the same path. Olga and Tanya had met Boris on the way home and told him that Ivan was missing. Boris then galloped full speed through the forest, searching for his son. He was much surprised to see him in the company of the Forest Ranger. He gave Ivan a bear hug—as all bears do!—and heard his story.

"You've shown me that humans and bears can not only work together, but live together like real friends," Boris told Peter. "They help each other out."

Olga and Tanya came running down the trail and caught up with the group. They smiled with relief to see Ivan safe and sound.

"Well, now that everyone is all right, I must hurry home," said Peter. Ivan did not want Peter to go. "Please join us for tea and raspberry jam!" he begged. "We will have a wonderful party."

But Peter explained that he was going home to his son Alexander—called Sasha for short—who was Ivan's age. "We live together, just the two of us," said Peter, his face turning sad. "Sasha is by himself much of the time. It's getting late now, and my son might be worried about me."

"Wait a minute, Peter. I want to show you something," Boris said. "Do you see that giant of a tree over there? It's an oak tree that is the oldest in the whole forest. It's a special tree. Come closer." Peter drew near the tree. "Now," Boris continued, "go around the tree three times."

Peter looked up at the oak. It had a trunk so big that even six people would have a hard time reaching their arms around it. Peter walked slowly around the trunk three times, stepping over enormous roots that looked like legs. Then he looked at Boris the Bear and saw that he was smiling.

"You are now a member of the Forest Family," Boris told the Forest Ranger. "From now on, you'll understand the language of all the forest creatures."

"Just listen to Robin Red Breast chat to his neighbors," Boris said. "He always is encouraging them to 'cheer up'!"

At first, Peter did not hear anything different. But then, instead of birds chirping, he heard the chatter of words. The forest was a chorus of voices. And Peter could understand every one!

The surprises of the forest were not over. Boris reached his paw into a deep hollow in the trunk of the giant oak tree and pulled out a chunk of wood.

"I hear you're good at wood carving," he told Peter. "There is a toy hidden in this piece of wood. Just take your knife and take away what shouldn't be there, and you will see the toy for yourself. The toy will do your son, Sasha, a lot of good."

That evening, after Sasha had gone to bed, Peter sat outside his front door and pulled out the chunk of wood and his carving knife. As he began to cut, he saw that Boris had been right: The figure seemed to carve itself. When he was finished, he held a small paddle, with a tiny wooden ball on strings suspended beneath. On top of the paddle was a wooden bear cub holding a small accordion. When Peter moved the paddle slowly in a circular motion, the little cub played his accordion.

Peter was happy. He had never carved anything so unusual before.

Early in the morning, while Sasha was still asleep, Peter put the wooden bear cub on his son's pillow. Then, very quietly, he slipped away to work.

When Sasha awoke, he almost knocked the toy to the floor. As he picked it up, he smiled. He was happy that his father had left him a surprise. As he held the toy, the ball that hung from the paddle began to sway, moving the carved bear. Suddenly, Sasha saw to his astonishment that the figure of the bear was coming to life.

It was little Ivan the bear cub! Ivan stood in the middle of the log cabin, with his accordion in his hands. Sasha could only stare, his mouth open in wonder. Sasha's dog Bimka was so surprised he did not even bark!

"Hello," said Ivan. "My father and yours have become friends. And now I want to be your friend. We are a family of magic bears in this magic forest."

"My father, Boris the Bear, told me that you are alone a lot. Now all you have to do is shake the wooden paddle when you want someone to play with, and I will appear before you. I'll take you to my house, and you can meet my family. We'll have tea, and I'll play the accordion and ask my father to sing songs."

"But how will we get to your home in the forest?" Sasha asked.

"Oh, that's easy now that you have a magic toy," Ivan said as he handed the wooden bear to Sasha. "Just close your eyes and move the paddle slowly in a circle. You will see what happens." Sasha did as Ivan instructed. Quicker than Bimka could wag his tail, Sasha and Ivan—and Bimka—were magically transported to the forest just outside the Bear Family's cabin. Sasha's pajamas had been transformed into clothes in the same blink of an eye.

There was Olga. There was Tanya. And there was Boris the Bear. On the table were bread and raspberry jam. Olga made tea and poured it for her guests from a large and beautiful pot, which the Siberians call a samovar.

They were having a party—and Sasha was the Guest of Honor. Even Sasha's dog, Bimka, got a piece of bread with a bit of jam on it. Nobody could resist giving table scraps to the little beggar!

"Daddy, Daddy," said Ivan. "I told our new friend, Sasha, that I would ask you to sing some songs for us. Will you? Please, Daddy, sing us a song about friendship, and I will play the accordion."

And so, until the sun set behind the mountains, all who passed near the cabin of the Bear Family heard laughter and music—and an occasional begging bark from the little dog named Bimka.

THE FRIENDSHIP SONG

WE'RE FRIENDS NOW. REMEMBER!
FRIENDS ARE FRIENDS FOREVER.
TO DO WHAT IT TAKES
THROUGH GOOD TIMES AND MISTAKES,
ALWAYS DO OUR BEST TO HELP A FRIEND—
THAT'S THE TEST.

WE'RE FRIENDS NOW. REMEMBER!
FRIENDS ARE FRIENDS FOREVER.
A FAMILY OF FRIENDS,
THE KIND THAT NEVER ENDS.
A FRIEND WILL GO FAR
TO FIND OUT HOW YOU ARE.

WE'RE FRIENDS NOW. REMEMBER!
FRIENDS ARE FRIENDS FOREVER.
TO BE THERE AND BE FAIR AND
SHOW A FRIEND YOU CARE.
WHEN YOU LEND A HELPING HAND,
YOU SHOW A FRIEND YOU UNDERSTAND.

WE'RE FRIENDS NOW. REMEMBER!
FRIENDS ARE FRIENDS FOREVER.
WE'RE FRIENDS NOW. REMEMBER!
FRIENDS ARE FRIENDS FOREVER.

FRIENDS NOW. REMEMBER!

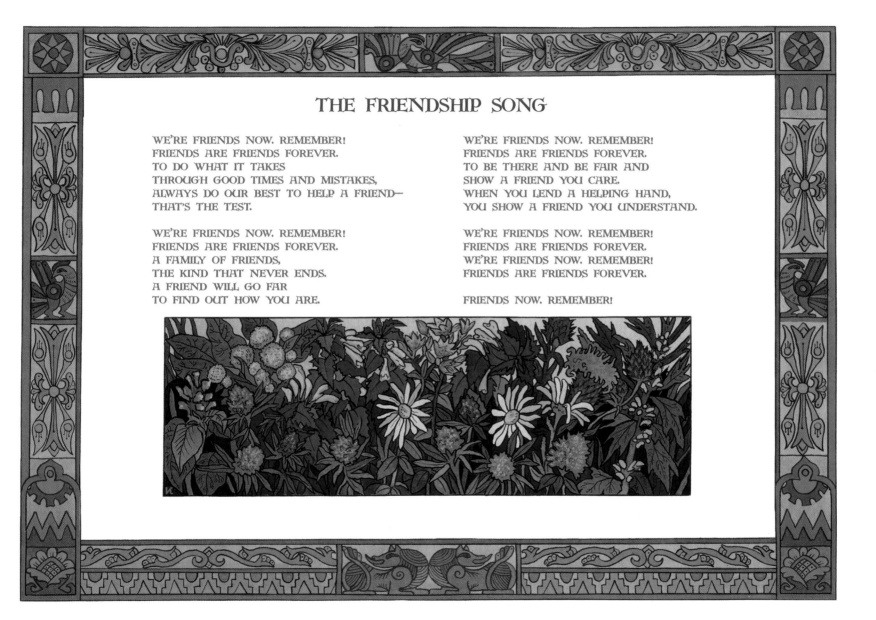

A NOTE ABOUT THE ART FOR PARENTS

This book is filled with symbols. Children and adults who look carefully at the illustrations can find all sorts of hidden meanings.

For example, the main characters in this modern-day fairytale are bears. People of Slavic origin consider bears to be among the most ancient of creatures. Slavs, the ancestors of the Russian people who now live in Siberia, once worshipped bears, praising them for their wisdom and strength.

In days past, Slavs decorated their clothes, utensils and homes with ornaments believed to protect against evil. Over time, magic gave way to aesthetics, as these ornaments began to serve a more decorative function. But the tradition of using ornament as symbol is still alive in Russian art. Following are some examples of this use in *The Four Bears*.

The ornamental borders of some of the illustrations reinforce the story's meaning through symbolism. On the title page, for example, the design at the bottom of the page is meant to evoke chaotic movement, symbolizing the disarray of the world when it is without a spiritual base. The S-patterned lines along the sides of the drawing symbolize the exaltation of the spirit, which results in harmony, or stability. This stability is shown in the central picture, which reflects the merger of spirit and reason into a harmonious union. The cones at the top of the drawing symbolize the fruit and seeds of this harmonious union.

The oak tree that Boris points out to Peter in the story is a symbol of the Tree of Life. The center ornament at the top and bottom of pages 28 and 29 show this oak as a woman, which in turn symbolizes the Mother of the World.

The two deer (page 55) symbolize the ties between the two worlds of Human and Animal.

The book's bright, lively and joyous colors are symbolic in their own way. They create an optimistic spirit and reflect the spiritual fruit of harmonious communication—friendship—between the human being and the animal.

An audiocassette of *The Four Bears* is available. Hear this fairytale come to life as you listen to the story read by a professional actor. The tape also includes original songs composed for *The Four Bears*.

Send $6.95, plus $3 for shipping and handling, to:

Boris the Bear, Inc.
P.O. Box 600
Roswell, GA 30075-9998